Colour CRACKERS

Read all the Colour CRACKERS books!

1 84121 244 X

1 84121 242 3

1 84121 232 6

1 84121 252 0

1 84121 258 X

1 84121 250 4

1 84121 228 8

1 84121 240 7

1 84121 238 5

1 84121 248 2

1 84121 256 3

1 84121 236 9

1 84121 246 6

1 84121 230 X

1 84121 234 2

1 84121 254 7

Pipe Down, Prudle!

The Most Talkative Parrot in the World!

Rose Impey
Shoo Rayner

ORCHARD BOOKS

ORCHARD BOOKS
96 Leonard Street, London EC2A 4XD
Orchard Books Australia
32/45-51 Huntley Street, Alexandria, NSW 2015
First published in Great Britain in 1995
This edition published in hardback in 2002
This edition published in paperback in 2003
Text © Rose Impey 1995
Illustrations © Shoo Rayner 2002
The rights of Rose Impey to be identified as the author
and Shoo Rayner as the illustrator of this work
have been asserted by them in accordance with the
Copyright, Designs and Patents Act, 1988.
A CIP catalogue record for this book is
available from the British Library.
ISBN 1 84121 880 4 (hardback)
ISBN 1 84121 250 4 (paperback)
1 3 5 7 9 10 8 6 4 2 (hardback)
3 5 7 9 10 8 6 4 2 (paperback)
Printed in China

Pipe Down, Prudle!

Not all parrots can talk.
Some parrots talk a lot.
Some parrots never know
when to stop.

How do you do?
How do you do?
I'm Prudle the parrot.
Pleased to meet you.

Prudle could talk
the leg off a donkey,

or the tail off a tom cat,

or the ears off an elephant.

Prudle was the most talkative
parrot in the world.

From the moment she woke up
Prudle never closed her beak.
She talked through breakfast

And when it came to bedtime
she was still talking.

Roll over!
Roll over!
Put the kettle on!

Sometimes she even talked
in her sleep.

Lights off!
Lights off!
Put the cat out!

"Pipe down, Prudle,"
everyone shouted.
But Prudle wouldn't.

Prudle belonged to Grandma Bates.
She was her pride and joy.
Grandma Bates taught Prudle to talk.

When she died, she left Prudle,
in her will,
to her grandson, Billy.

But Billy wasn't pleased
to meet Prudle.
Nor was his family.
The Bates family didn't like birds.
They liked television.

They didn't like it
when Prudle talked through
Blue Peter

and *EastEnders*

18

and *Coronation Street.*

She *tried* to talk through *Top of the Pops.*

"Someone switch that parrot off,"
said Billy Bates.
"I wish we could," said Mrs Bates.
"Pipe down, Prudle," said the girls.
But Prudle wouldn't.

She talked when Billy Bates
was trying to have a nap…

Wake up! Wake up!
Car needs a clean.

when his wife was having
coffee with a neighbour…

when Bonnie was playing with her friends…

when Becky had her boyfriend round.

Soon the whole family agreed,
"That parrot will have to go!"

But Prudle liked living
with the Bates family.
No matter how hard they tried
they couldn't get rid of her.

In the end, they found one way
of keeping her quiet.

But one day the Bates family
were glad they couldn't
silence Prudle.
Very glad indeed.

It was a Monday morning.
Mr and Mrs Bates
were late for work.
Bonnie and Becky were late
for school.
The family went out
in such a rush
they left Prudle covered up.

The house was quiet.
The whole street was quiet.
Even Prudle was quiet for a change.
She was still asleep.

Suddenly *someone* put his hand
round the window
and let himself in.

Someone else followed him in.
They were definitely up to no good.

The burglars looked around
to see what they could steal.
They stole Billy Bates's
snooker cups.

They stole Mrs Bates's watch
and the family camera.

Smile!

They stole Bonnie's computer
and Becky's stereo.

And, as if that wasn't bad enough,
they stole the Bates' television!

They piled them all up
inside the front door.
"Just got time for a drink,"
said the first burglar.
"Coffee or tea?" said the second.
"Hot chocolate," said the first.

The burglars put on the radio
while they had their snack.
The radio woke Prudle up.

The burglars were amazed.
They didn't know where
the noise was coming from.
"Come on, Stan,"
said the first burglar.
"This place gives me the creeps."

"And me, Sid," said the second burglar. "I'm off."

The burglars picked up
the things they had stolen.
They opened the front door
and tried to sneak out.
But Prudle started up again.

The burglars were scared.
"Quick, Stan, you take the telly,"
said Sid.
"Right, Sid. Let's get out of here,"
said Stan, "before the coppers come."

Sid and Stan drove off
in a big red van.
It was full of stolen things.
They had burgled half the houses
in the street.
When everyone came home from work
there was such a fuss.

The police came round.
They took down the details.
They looked for clues
and fingerprints.
"We'll try to find them,"
said the policeman.
But he wasn't very hopeful.

The Bates family was fed up.
Becky had no stereo to listen to.
Bonnie had no computer to play on.
But, worst of all,
they had no television to watch.
The whole family sat there
with nothing to do
and nothing to say.

Except for Prudle of course.
They couldn't keep her quiet.

For a moment there was silence
then Prudle started up again.

This place gives me the creeps.
Gives me the creeps.

The policeman took Prudle's statement.

Sid and Stan were very sorry that
they had burgled the Bates' house.
They were sorry
they had stopped there
for a drink
and a rest.

They had a long time in prison
to feel sorry about it.

After that Prudle was very popular
with the Bates family
and with all their neighbours.
No one tried to keep her quiet now.
In fact, Prudle always had someone
to talk to.

Did I ever tell
you about the time I
caught two burglars?
Two burglars!
My name's Prudle.
I'm famous.

Crack-A-Joke

Why did the robber cut
the legs off his bed?
He wanted to lie low for a while!

What do you use to stuff a parrot?
Polly-filla!

What did the
policeman say
to his tummy?
**You're under
a vest!**

What happened to the burglar who stole a bar of soap?
He made a clean getaway!

What three letters frighten robbers?
I.C.U.

There are 16 Colour Crackers books.
Collect them all!

❏ A Birthday for Bluebell   1 84121 228 8   £3.99
❏ A Fortune for Yo-Yo   1 84121 230 X   £3.99
❏ A Medal for Poppy   1 84121 244 X   £3.99
❏ Hot Dog Harris   1 84121 232 6   £3.99
❏ Long Live Roberto   1 84121 246 6   £3.99
❏ Open Wide, Wilbur   1 84121 248 2   £3.99
❏ Phew, Sidney!   1 84121 234 2   £3.99
❏ Pipe Down, Prudle!   1 84121 250 4   £3.99
❏ Precious Potter   1 84121 236 9   £3.99
❏ Rhode Island Roy   1 84121 252 0   £3.99
❏ Sleepy Sammy   1 84121 238 5   £3.99
❏ Stella's Staying Put   1 84121 254 7   £3.99
❏ Tiny Tim   1 84121 240 7   £3.99
❏ Too Many Babies   1 84121 242 3   £3.99
❏ We Want William!   1 84121 256 3   £3.99
❏ Welcome Home, Barney   1 84121 258 X   £3.99

Colour Crackers are available from all good bookshops,
or can be ordered direct from the publisher:
Orchard Books, PO BOX 29, Douglas IM99 1BQ
Credit card orders please telephone 01624 836000 or fax 01624 837033
or e-mail: bookshop@enterprise.net for details.
To order please quote title, author and ISBN and your full name and address.
Cheques and postal orders should be made payable to 'Bookpost plc'.
Postage and packing is FREE within the UK
(overseas customers should add £1.00 per book).
Prices and availability are subject to change.

1 84121 244 X

1 84121 240 7

1 84121 238 5

1 84121 252 0

1 84121 256 3

1 84121 236 9

1 84121 228 8

1 84121 230 X

1 84121 234 2

1 84121 248 2

1 84121 242 3

1 84121 232 6

1 84121 246 6

1 84121 258 X

1 84121 250 4

1 84121 254 7

Read all the Colour CRACKERS books!

Collect all the
Colour Crackers!